The Bull and the Fire Truck

by **Tony Johnston**
Illustrated by **R.W. Alley**

Hello Reader! — Level 3

SCHOLASTIC INC.
New York Toronto London Auckland Sydney

A NOTE TO PARENTS

Reading Aloud with Your Child
Research shows that reading books aloud is the single most valuable support parents can provide in helping children learn to read.

- Be a ham! The more enthusiasm you display, the more your child will enjoy the book.
- Run your finger underneath the words as you read to signal that the print carries the story.
- Leave time for examining the illustrations more closely; encourage your child to find things in the pictures.
- Invite your youngster to join in whenever there's a repeated phrase in the text.
- Link up events in the book with similar events in your child's life.
- If your child asks a question, stop and answer it. The book can be a means to learning more about your child's thoughts.

Listening to Your Child Read Aloud
The support of your attention and praise is absolutely crucial to your child's continuing efforts to learn to read.

- If your child is learning to read and asks for a word, give it immediately so that the meaning of the story is not interrupted. DO NOT ask your child to sound out the word.
- On the other hand, if your child initiates the act of sounding out, don't intervene.
- If your child is reading along and makes what is called a miscue, listen for the sense of the miscue. If the word "road" is substituted for the word "street," for instance, no meaning is lost. Don't stop the reading for a correction.
- If the miscue makes no sense (for example, "horse" for "house"), ask your child to reread the sentence because you're not sure you understand what's just been read.
- Above all else, enjoy your child's growing command of print and make sure you give lots of praise. *You are your child's first teacher — and the most important one. Praise from you is critical for further risk-taking and learning.*

— Priscilla Lynch
Ph.D., New York University
Educational Consultant

For Samantha, my "neglected middle child"
—T.J.

To the little people and the big people at
Barrington Early Childhood Center
—R.W.A.

Bad Decision

A bull saw something red.
He gored it.
It was a fire truck.
He should have ignored it.
—T. Johnston

Text copyright © 1996 by Tony Johnston.
Illustrations copyright © 1996 by R.W. Alley.
All rights reserved. Published by Scholastic Inc.
HELLO READER!, CARTWHEEL BOOKS, and the CARTWHEEL BOOKS logo are
registered trademarks of Scholastic Inc.

Library of Congress Cataloging-in-Publication Data
Johnston, Tony.
    The bull and the fire truck / by Tony Johnston ; illustrated by R.W. Alley.
       p.   cm.—(Hello reader! Level 3)
    Summary: A big, bulky, brave bull named Bernardo is infuriated by anything
red.
    ISBN 0-590-47597-5
    [1. Bulls—Fiction. 2. Red—Fiction. 3. Fire engines—Fiction.]
I. Alley, R.W. (Robert W.), ill. II. Title. III. Series.
PZ7.J6478Bu 1996
[E]—dc20
                                      95-30064
                                          CIP
                                          AC

12 11 10 9 8 7 6 5 4 3 2 1   6 7 8 9/9 0 1/0
Printed in the U.S.A.   23
First Scholastic printing, October 1996

Bernardo was a bull, big and bulky
and brave. He lived with his family on
a farm. But one day he was driven
to a new farm in a bright red truck.

The red truck made him mad. It was like
a cage. On the trip, he snorted at it. He tried
to shake it. He tried to butt its red sides.
But he was too big and bulky to move.

From then on, Bernardo did not
like red. Red apples, red flowers,
red bandannas. Red made him mad.

Bernardo roamed the fields of his new
home, eating grass and growing bigger
and bulkier.

One day he heard something.
Cling! Cling! Clang! Clang!
WHEEEEEEEEE! A bright red
fire truck, rushing to a fire,
sped past Bernardo's field.

The fire truck made him think of
the other red truck. It made him mad.
So he stopped chewing grass and
started chasing the fire truck.

When it reached the town, the fire truck slowed down for cars. Bernardo did not slow down. Big and bulky and brave, he charged full speed ahead.

Wham! Wham! Wham! He tried to smash it.

The fire fighters could not believe their eyes. They were thrown all around like hay. Most of all, they were surprised.

"Stop! Stop! Stop!" they shouted.

But Bernardo kept butting the fire truck. *Pound! Pound! Pound!*

Hoses snaked all over the street. Pieces rattled to the ground.

People crowded around when they heard the loud sounds.

Bernardo's owner drove by.

"Stop! Stop! Stop!" He shouted at Bernardo. But Bernardo was big and bulky and brave. He did not stop till he knocked himself silly.

The fire truck was dented like a big tin can. A tow truck took it away.

Another fire truck went to the fire.

Bernardo and the fire fighters went to the doctor.

The fire fighters had some bumps, but they were fine.

Bernardo had some bumps, too. Mostly, his head hurt.

"What happened?" the doctor asked
Bernardo's owner.
"My bull hates red," the farmer said.
"So he wrecked a fire truck."

The doctor smiled. "He's sure got spunk."
He gave Bernardo a pat. He gave the
farmer a note: *Keep this bull away from red!*

So the farmer put Bernardo in a far field where there was nothing red to make him mad. To be extra safe, he grew yellow apples, planted blue flowers, wore a purple bandanna, and—he painted his truck green.

"Good idea," said the fire fighters.
They painted their truck green, too.